A Note to Parents and Caregivers:

Read-it! Readers are for children who are just starting on the amazing road to reading. These beautiful books support both the acquisition of reading skills and the love of books.

The PURPLE LEVEL presents basic topics and objects using high frequency words and simple language patterns.

The RED LEVEL presents familiar topics using common words and repeating sentence patterns.

The BLUE LEVEL presents new ideas using a larger vocabulary and varied sentence structure.

The YELLOW LEVEL presents more challenging ideas, a broad vocabulary, and wide variety in sentence structure.

The GREEN LEVEL presents more complex ideas, an extended vocabulary range, and expanded language structures.

The ORANGE LEVEL presents a wide range of ideas and concepts using challenging vocabulary and complex language structures.

When sharing a book with your child, read in short stretches, pausing often to talk about the pictures. Have your child turn the pages and point to the pictures and familiar words. And be sure to reread favorite stories or parts of stories.

There is no right or wrong way to share books with children. Find time to read with your child, and pass on the legacy of literacy.

Adria F. Klein, Ph.D.
Professor Emeritus
California State University
San Bernardino, California

For Geraye, for sharing more than 35 years of laughter with me—J.K.

Editors: Christianne Jones and Julie Gassman
Designer: Hilary Wacholz
Art Director: Heather Kindseth
The illustrations in this book were created with watercolor and pen.

Picture Window Books
5115 Excelsior Boulevard
Suite 232
Minneapolis, MN 55416
877-845-8392
www.picturewindowbooks.com

All books published by Picture Window Books
are manufactured with paper containing at least
10 percent post-consumer waste.

Library of Congress Cataloging-in-Publication Data
Kalz, Jill.
Tuckerbean on the moon / by Jill Kalz ; illustrated by Benton Mahan.
p. cm. — (Read-it! readers)
ISBN 978-1-4048-5234-1
[1. Space flight to the moon—Fiction. 2. Moon—Fiction. 3. Dogs—Fiction.]
I. Mahan, Ben, ill. II. Title.
PZ7.K12655Tuf 2009
[E]—dc22
                                        2008031250

Tuckerbean
on the Moon

by Jill Kalz
illustrated by Benton Mahan

Special thanks to our reading adviser:

Adria F. Klein, Ph.D.
Professor Emeritus, California State University
San Bernardino, California

PICTURE WINDOW BOOKS
Minneapolis, Minnesota

4

Tuckerbean likes to look at the stars. He smiles at them when they twinkle.

The moon grins. Tuckerbean winks.
Tonight he is taking a long,
special trip.

The space center is bright and busy. A rocket stands tall. A giant clock counts down to liftoff.

Tuckerbean is going to the moon!

9

Inside the rocket, Tuckerbean pushes buttons. He flips switches. He hums a silly song. Everyone giggles.

Three … two … one … blastoff!
The rocket zooms. It wobbles
and shakes.

Tuckerbean floats like a balloon.

When the rocket lands, Tuckerbean and his crew jump out. They have a parade.

Tuckerbean lies in the moon dust.
He makes moon angels.

Tuckerbean climbs into his moon buggy. He races over the hills.

Tuckerbean takes pictures.
He writes postcards that say
"Hello from the moon!"

On the way back home, Tuckerbean sees stars. He waves at them when they twinkle.

More *Read-it!* Readers

Bright pictures and fun stories help you practice your reading skills. Look for more books at your level.

Bears on Ice
The Bossy Rooster
The Camping Scare
Dust Bunnies
Emily's Pictures
Flying with Oliver
Frog Pajama Party
Galen's Camera
Greg Gets a Hint
The Kickball Game
Last in Line

The Lifeguard
Mike's Night-light
Nate the Dinosaur
One Up for Brad
Pup's Prairie Home
Robin's New Glasses
The Sassy Monkey
The Treasure Map
Tuckerbean
What's Bugging Pamela?

On the Web

FactHound offers a safe, fun way to find Web sites related to this book. All of the sites on FactHound have been researched by our staff.

1. Visit *www.facthound.com*

2. Type in this special code:
   1404852344

3. Click on the FETCH IT button.

Your trusty FactHound will fetch the best sites for you! A complete list of *Read-it!* Readers is available on our Web site:
www.picturewindowbooks.com